My hair is so BIG!
That I cant wear a
hat.

My hair is so BIG!
That's it's a bed for
my Cat.

My hair is so BIG!
That brushing it is
tough.

And one bottle of shampoo is never enough.

My hair is so BIG!
That it takes
forever to dry.

But when it finally dries it reaches up to the sky.
B

My hair is so BIG
that everyone
stares.

And they always
ask me questions
like, is that your
real hair?

Everyone wants to touch my hair, just to see how it feels.

BREAKING NEWS
My Big Big hair is a Really BIG DEAL.

They always ask
me questions like
How did you get
your hair that way
we all would love
to know ?
I'd just shrug my
shoulders and say
that's just the way
it grows •
B
3

GEL
My Big hair has its challenges everyday.

But I love my Big Big BIG HAIR!!! I wouldn't have It any other way.

BREAKING NEWS
My Big Big hair is a Really BIG DEAL.

BREAKING NEWS
My Big Big hair is a Really BIG DEAL.

BREAKING NEWS
My Big Big hair is a Really BIG DEAL.

GEL
My Big hair has its challenges everyday.

But I love my Big
Big BIG HAIR!!! I
wouldn't have It
any other way.

But when it finally
dries it reaches up
to the sky.

But when it finally
dries it reaches up
to the sky.
IB

But when it finally
dries it reaches up
to the sky.

They always ask
me questions like
How did you get
your hair that way
we all would love
to know ?
I'd just shrug my
shoulders and say
that's just the way
it grows •
B
3

They always ask me questions like How did you get your hair that way we all would love to know ?
B
3
I'd just shrug my shoulders and say that's just the way it grows .

They always ask
me questions like
How did you get
your hair that way
we all would love
to know ?
I'd just shrug my
shoulders and say
that's just the way
it grows •

They always ask
me questions like
How did you get
your hair that way
we all would love
to know ?
B
3
I'd just shrug my
shoulders and say
that's just the way
it grows .

They always ask me questions like How did you get your hair that way we all would love to know ?
I'd just shrug my shoulders and say that's just the way it grows •
B
3

Made in the USA
Columbia, SC
16 July 2020

13991077R00015